THE STORY OF PETER PAN

With the spring comes Wendy

THE STORY OF PETER PAN

RETOLD FROM THE FAIRY PLAY BY SIR J.M.BARRIE
BY DANIEL O'CONNOR

ILLUSTRATED BY ALICE B.WOODWARD

LONDON
G. BELL & SONS LTD
1931

Octavo Edition, First Issued, November 1914
Reprinted, December 1914 (twice); January 1915;
    May 1915; September 1915; January 1916;
    March 1916; November 1916; November 1917;
    May 1918; February 1919; April 1920;
    December 1921
New Edition, with additional Colour-plates, July 1922
Reprinted July 1923; September 1924
New Edition reset, with additional illustrations,
    September 1926; Reprinted, August 1927;
    March 1929; January 1931.

PRINTED IN GREAT BRITAIN BY
PURNELL AND SONS, PAULTON (SOMERSET) AND LONDON

PREFACE

SIR J. M. BARRIE'S delightful creation, "Peter Pan," has by this time taken a secure place in the hearts of children of all ages, and there are few nurseries in the land in which Peter, Wendy, Tinker Bell, Captain Hook and his Pirates, the Mermaids and Redskins, and the exciting world in which they lived, are not as familiar as the most time-honoured lore of fairyland.

The popularity of Mr. Daniel O'Connor's version of the story, issued with Sir J. M. Barrie's kind consent, and illustrated so charmingly by Miss Alice B. Woodward, has induced the publishers to bring out the present re-issue at a lower price.

The selections of music which will be found in it are included with the permission of Mr. John Crook, the composer, and Messrs. Price and Reynolds.

CONTENTS

LIST OF ILLUSTRATIONS

PART I
EARLY DAYS

LULLABY

Gold - en slum - bers kiss your eyes,
Smiles a - wake you when you rise, Sleep, pret - ty dar - ling,
do not cry, And I will sing a lul - la - by.

THE STORY
OF PETER PAN

EARLY DAYS

IN one of the nicest nurseries in the world there were beds for three young people called John Napoleon, and Wendy Moira Angela, and Michael, the children of Mr. and Mrs. Darling. The nursery was wide and airy, with a large window, and a bright fire with a high fire-guard round it, and a big clock, and prettily-coloured nursery-rhyme pictures over the walls. It was in many ways a most interesting household. For one thing, although there was a pretty little parlour-maid called Liza, the children were bathed and dressed by a big dog called Nana, whose kennel was kept in the nursery.

On the evening on which our story begins, Nana was dozing peacefully by the fireside, with her head between her paws. Mr. and Mrs. Darling were getting ready to go out to dinner and Nana was to be left in sole charge of the children. Presently the clock went off with a whirr, and struck—one, two, three, four, five, six—time to begin to put the children to bed.

Nana got up, and stretched herself, and carefully switched on the electric light. You would have been surprised to see how cleverly she managed to do that with her mouth. Then she turned the bedclothes neatly down and hung the little pyjamas over the fire-guard. She then trotted up to the bathroom and turned on the water; after feeling it with her paw to make sure that it was not too hot, she went off to look for Michael, who, being the youngest of the three children, must go to bed first. She returned immediately with him sitting astride on her back as though she were a pony. Michael, of course, did not want to be bathed, but Nana was firm and, taking him to the bathroom, shut the door so that he should not be in a draught. Then Mrs. Darling came to peep at him as he splashed about in the nice warm water.

Whilst Mrs. Darling was in the nursery she heard a wee noise outside the window, as a tiny figure, no bigger than a little boy, tried the window-latch, and vanished suddenly at her cry of surprise. She flung the window open, but there was nothing to be seen, nothing but the dim roofs of the neighbouring houses, and the deep blue sky above. She began to

frighten herself with eerie bogie tales, for the same thing had happened the day before, when Nana had gone to the window and shut it down so quickly that she had cut off the boy's shadow. Mrs. Darling had found it in Nana's mouth, and had carefully folded it and put it away.

But she soon felt reassured when her children came in together in answer to her call. John Napoleon and Wendy were playing at their favourite game of being Father and Mother, and Mrs. Darling's beautiful face beamed with delight as she listened to them. Suddenly, in rushed Mr. Darling, very much excited because he

With Michael sitting on her back

could see of her was the little flame, but
you could *hear* her distinctly, she made a
tinkling noise like a little silver bell, and
that was why she was called Tinker Bell.
Tinker Bell at last rested a few moments
on the second drawer of the nursery
dresser; instantly the boy ran joyfully to
it, and pulling open the drawer snatched
out his shadow neatly rolled up, just as
Mrs. Darling had left it. He had found
it certainly, but the next trouble was to
put it on again. A happy thought struck
him; he would stick it on with soap!
Sitting on the hearthrug, he soaped his
feet and then he soaped his shadow, but
whichever way he soaped they would not
stick together. There is no
use in having a shadow if it will
not stick to you. After trying
and trying in
vain the poor
little fellow
gave up the

attempt, buried his face in his hands, and sobbed despairingly.

It was then that Wendy awoke. She sat right up in bed, and, not at all frightened, said: " Little boy, why are you crying? "

The elfin creature sprang to his feet, and taking off his cap, bowed very politely. Wendy curtsied in return, though she found it a difficult thing to do in bed.

" What's your name? " asked the little boy.

" Wendy Moira Angela Darling. What's yours? "

" Peter Pan."

" Where do you live? "

" Second turning to the right, and straight on till morning."

This seemed to Wendy a very funny address, but she was all sympathy when she heard that Peter had no mother. No wonder he was crying! But that was not the reason for Peter's tears; he was crying know what a kiss was, but being a nice little girl of motherly disposition, she did not hurt his feelings by laughing at him, but simply placed the thimble on his finger.

Peter admired the thimble very much. " Shall I give you a kiss? " he asked and, jerking a button off his coat, solemnly presented it to her.

Wendy at once fastened it on a chain which she wore round her neck, and, forgetting the puzzle in his mind, she once more asked him for a kiss.

Immediately he returned the thimble. " Oh! I didn't mean a *kiss,* I meant a thimble! "

" What's that? " he asked.

" It's like this," replied Wendy, and gently kissed his cheek.

" Oh! " cried Peter, " how nice! " and he began to give her *thimbles* in return, and ever afterwards he called a kiss a thimble, and a thimble a kiss.

" But Peter, how old are you? " continued Wendy.

" I don't know, but quite young. I ran away the day I was born."

" Ran away—why? "

" Because I heard my father and mother talking about what I was to be when I became a man. I don't want to be a man. I want always to be a little boy and have fun. So I ran away and lived among the fairies."

Wendy was almost speechless with delight at the thought of sitting beside a boy who knew fairies, and after a minute said: " Peter, do you really know fairies? "

" Yes, but they're nearly all dead now. You see, Wendy, when the first baby laughed for the first time, its laugh broke into a thousand pieces, and they all went skipping about, and that was the begin-

Wendy gently kissed his cheek

ning of fairies. And now, whenever a new
baby is born, its first laugh becomes a
fairy. So there ought to be a fairy for
every little boy and girl, but there isn't.
You see children know such a lot now.
They soon won't believe in fairies, and
whenever a child says: ' I don't believe
in fairies,' there's a fairy somewhere that
falls down dead."

Peter suddenly looked about the room,
as though he were searching for something. Tinker Bell had disappeared!
Before he could grow anxious, however,
a tinkling of bells was heard, and Peter,
who knew the fairy language, of course
understood it. He pulled open the
drawer in which his shadow had been
hidden, and out sprang Tinker Bell, very
angry with him for shutting her up acci-
dentally in the drawer. She skipped about
the room, but Wendy gave such a cry of
delight that Tink was frightened and hid
behind the clock.

" But Peter," continued Wendy, " if you don't live with the fairies, where do you live? "

" I live with the Lost Boys."

" Who are they? "

" Why, they are the children who fall out of their peram- bulators when their nurses are looking the other way. If they are not claimed within seven days, they are sent far away to the Never-Never- Never Land to defray expenses. I'm their Captain."

" Oh! what fun! But, Peter, why did you come to our nursery window? "

Peter told her that he came to listen to the lovely stories Wendy's mother related to her children, for the Lost Boys

had no mothers, and no one to tell them
any stories. He also told her how he led
them against their enemies, the pirates and
the wolves, and how they enjoyed bathing
in the Lagoon, where beautiful mermaids
sang and swam all day long.

" I must go back now," he went on,
" the boys will be anxious to hear the end
of the story about the Prince and the
Glass Slipper. I told them as much as I
knew, and they're longing to hear the
rest."

Wendy begged him to stay.

" I'll tell you lots more," she promised,
" ever so many stories if you'll only
stay."

" Come, Wendy! " exclaimed Peter,
struck with a new idea. " You can tell
us all the stories there, and darn our
clothes, and tuck us in at night. None of
us has ever been tucked in. All the boys
long for a mother. Oh, Wendy, do
come! "

It was a tempting idea to Wendy, but a sudden thought came across her mind. " Peter, I can't! Think of Mummy! Besides, I can't fly."

" I'll teach you, Wendy."

This was too much for her. " Peter, will you teach John and Michael to fly as well? "

" Yes, if you like."

So John and Michael were awakened, and directly they heard that there were pirates in the Never-Never-Never Land they began to clamour to go at once. They watched Peter fly about the room, and tried to imitate him, flapping their arms clumsily at first like unfledged birds, and flopping about all over the place.

" That will never do," Peter said, " I must blow the fairy dust on you. Now waggle your shoulders as I do."

So they tried, and found that they could fly; just a little at first, from the bed to the floor and back again; then over the bed and across the room, and then, as they grew braver, almost as freely and easily as Peter himself.

" Tink, lead the way! " called Peter, and the fairy shot out like a little star. None of the children had time to put on their day clothes, but John snatched his top hat as he flew out of the window, followed by Michael. Peter Pan held Wendy's hand, and away they floated into the dark blue depths of the starry night.

A minute afterwards Mrs. Darling, who had just returned from the party, rushed into the nursery with Nana at her heels, for Nana had been anxious about her charges, and had just succeeded in breaking her chain. But it was too late. The children were already on their way to the Never-Never-Never Land.

AWAY THEY FLOATED

THE NEVER-NEVER-NEVER LAND

FAR away in the Never-Never-Never Land the Lost Boys lived in the depths of the forest, on the banks of a lake now covered with ice. The trees were bare without their summer dress, and wolves prowled and howled in the distance, and wild beasts snarled in the undergrowth, and Pirates sailed villainously up the lake, and Red Indians, who were friends of the boys, lived secretly in their wigwams hidden in the glades of the woods.

The Lost Boys, who, in their fur coats, looked more like bears than boys, were anxiously awaiting Peter's return. There

were six of them: Slightly Soiled, the
eldest; then came Tootles, and Nibs, and
Curly, and the Twins, who were so much
alike that one name did for both of them,
so each was called Twin. They lived
like moles under the ground, for fear of
the Pirates and the wolves.   Each one had

a special staircase hollowed in a tree-
trunk, so that they could easily run down
among the roots of the trees into their
home. They were playing about happily,
although they were beginning to be a
little anxious that Peter was so long away.
Slightly was tootling on a whistle, and
dancing quite merrily, with an ostrich for
partner (a queer companion, you will say),

crocodile was asleep, and with that and a swift ship he had managed so far to escape. It was an awful life!

Fortunately for Hook, the crocodile had once, in an ill-advised moment, swallowed an alarum clock (one of those patent ninety-nine-years clocks, warranted to go any time, anywhere and anyhow). Go it did, and it ticked so loudly that the Captain could always hear it coming, and it was the signal for him to bolt!

Hook sat down on one of the enormous forest mushrooms (in the Never-Never-Never Land mushrooms grow to a gigantic size) to deliberate about his mode of revenge. He was in the middle of a torrent of braggings and boastings when he felt his seat getting not only warm, but much too warm, and little wonder in that, for when he furiously leapt up he found that he had really been sitting on a chimney of the underground home which Peter had cleverly disguised.

He realised at once that the Lost Boys must be living in safety down below.

Very soon he had a wicked, treacherous plan settled. He determined to cook a huge rich cake, with beautiful green icing and a poisoned inside. He was sure that the Lost Boys, who had no mother to look after them, would eat it greedily, and die with awful pains inside. Smee, as the Captain's wily lieutenant was called, was overjoyed at this plan, and chuckled loudly.

"Shake hands on't," said Hook, but Smee did not want to, and begged to be excused.

"Paw, Smee, paw," said the Captain in an awful voice, so Smee had to take the horrid hook in his hand, and they both

"THE CROCODILE! THE CROCODILE!"

danced round while Hook sang with diabolical grimaces:

> "Yo ho, yo ho, when I say 'Paw'
>   By fear they're overtook;
> Naught's left upon your bones when you
>   Have shaken hands with Hook."

Just as he was gloating over his pleasant scheme a queer sound was heard, like a corncrake coming nearer and nearer through a barley field. " Tick, tack, tick, tack, tick, tack."

" The Crocodile! the Crocodile! " the Pirate Captain yelled, and in a moment was flying for his life.

The Pirates had scarcely disappeared in the depths of the forest when the Indians crept silently up in pursuit of them. Tiger Lily, their chieftainess, was at their head, now running swiftly under the trees, now listening with her ear to the ground, to know where her enemies had gone. For, like Tinker Bell and Wendy, she loved

Peter Pan, and his enemies were her enemies.

The Redskins slid along, following the Pirates with steps as quiet as those of a beetle crawling through the grass. They soon passed far out of sight, and then, one by one, the Lost Boys peeped from their tree-trunks and, seeing that all was quiet, came out again to their playground in the woods.

But their safety did not last for long. A fierce barking of wolves was heard, and Nibs, who had gone off by himself, rushed, quite out of breath, into the midst of the Boys, closely pursued by a pack of lean and hungry wolves with glittering fiery eyes. What were the Lost Boys to do in this terrible plight, when their leader was far away? Fortunately, one of them remembered Peter's plan. Whenever he was attacked by wild beasts Peter used to run at them backwards, jumping along the ground, squinting at them through his legs.

THE INDIANS CREPT SILENTLY UP

The lost boys knelt before her

only Peter would be Father, and that now, if they liked to come in, she would tell them the story of Cinderella.

In they bundled, one after the other, to listen to the tale. And they were so big, and the house was so small, that they must have been packed like sardines inside. But a sort of cosy feeling like that

was, I expect, just what they wanted, and they were very happy.

The evening fell softly down on the forest, and the shadows rose, so that everything was dark and still, save for the occasional baying of a wolf. Lights were lit in the little house, and at last, when it was quite night,

D

Peter came out with his sword, and walked up and down like a sentry, to guard the new little mother he had brought for the Lost Boys.

PART III

THE MERMAIDS' LAGOON

SHE WAS COMBING HER LONG TRESSES

THE MERMAIDS' LAGOON

ONE fine summer evening Peter, with
Wendy and their little family, went
down to the Lagoon where the Mermaids
lived. The Never-Never-Never Land,
as you see, is full of the most strange and
interesting creatures; some of them dreadful, like the Pirates, wolves, and croco-
diles; others, like the fairies and the
mermaids, altogether beautiful and charming. Wendy and her brothers, who had
never seen a real mermaid with a tail,
were very much excited, and, as luck
would have it, just as they arrived at the

lagoon, one of them, seated on a rock, was combing her long tresses, on which the sunlight gleamed, until they shone like a mixture of gold and bronze, for they had a beautiful greenish tinge. As she combed her hair she sang such a wonderful melody that the boys longed to catch her. They instantly dashed into the water, but with a piercing cry of " Mortals! " the Mermaid dived out of their reach into the lowest depths.

" But look! here is another little mermaid! Surely we can catch her! " said John Napoleon Darling, and he very nearly did. Mermaids, however, are hard to catch, and when caught, are still harder to hold. John succeeded in getting the little sprite in his hands but, wriggling

A FIERCE FIGHT ENSUED

and they were both in great danger. As he watched the water silently creeping nearer, Peter almost despaired. But all at once a large kite came flying slowly over the lagoon. In a second Peter had seized its tail, and binding it tightly round Wendy, he sent her sailing away in safety, bravely calling, "Good-bye Wendy!" until she was out of sight.

Then indeed, as the tide rose steadily, Peter was in great peril. The water reached his feet, and he was beginning to think it would be a "tremendous adventure to die," when who should come sailing by but a great sea-bird on its nest, which had been blown off the cliffs by the rising storm. "Hurrah!" cried Peter, "there's a lovely boat for me!" and chasing the bird off, in he stepped, curled himself round and, spreading out his coat to the wind, sailed swiftly and merrily after Wendy.

Spreading his coat to the wind, he sailed merrily

PART IV

THE UNDERGROUND HOME

THE UNDERGROUND HOME

THE days passed merrily in the underground home, where Wendy was the sweetest little mother, and Peter the bravest father you could ever have found anywhere. The cave was large and roomy, and the rocks out of which it was hollowed were of a deep brown colour. There was a fine large fireplace, and overhead, near the ceiling, were hung baskets and fishing-tackle and all sorts of things likely to be useful to cave-dwellers.

Wendy had not been long there before she had improved the home and made it as comfortable as her own nursery. It is wonderful what clever girls can do, even with the poorest materials. There was now a huge bed for all the Boys, and a basket for Michael, because he was the littlest and because a cradle is such a homely thing to have about the house. And in a corner of the room, hidden behind a tiny crimson curtain, there was a wee little room for Tinker Bell, daintily furnished to suit the tastes of a girl fairy. There were stools made of mushrooms for the Boys, and two comfortable chairs made of pumpkins, where Peter and Wendy could sit in state, as was fitting the father and mother of the little family.

One Saturday night, Wendy and the Boys were all downstairs together, waiting for Peter to come back from a hunting expedition. Outside, the faithful Tiger Lily and her Red Indian band were keeping guard against the Pirates.

Presently the crackling of branches indicated Peter's approach through the underwood. Tiger Lily sprang up to meet him, and the Lost Boys ran to the tree-trunk stairways to welcome him on his return. He was the best of fathers; and never forgot to be a little boy, for he had filled his pockets with fruit for the boys who had been good, and he let them rummage through and through his coat like rats in a corn sack.

Then he turned towards Wendy, who was very busy mending the children's socks by the fireside. She looked very charming in her pretty brown frock the colour of autumn leaves, with scarlet berries in her hair, and she made Peter very happy as they exchanged thimbles and talked over the boys and their doings as if they had really been their father and mother. When the children clamoured for a dance, Peter even said that he was too old for such a game, and that his old bones would simply rattle, and Wendy also thought that the mother of such an armful could not go skipping about with her children. So Peter sang " Sally in our Alley," which song Wendy thought no one else in all the world could sing so sweetly as the darling of her heart, while the others danced pillow dances, and bolster dances, and turned somersaults on the beds, and did all the other jolly and lively things that everyone wants to do just about bedtime, when one ought to be thinking of going to sleep.

At last they quietened down for Wendy to tell them just one more story before they were tucked in for the night. They clustered eagerly round, interrupting every sentence, as children always do, even the best of them, while Wendy told her story. And the story somehow seemed familiar to John, and Michael, and Peter, for it was the tale of Mr. and Mrs. Darling, poor dears, who had lost their children one winter night; and how sad they were about it, how lonely they felt, and how the nursery window would always be kept open, ready for the children, if ever they should come flying home again.

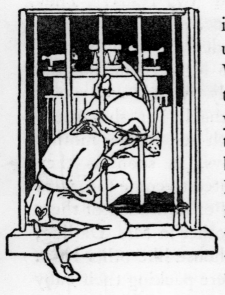

When she had finished, Peter stood up sadly. "No, Wendy," he said, "I thought so once, but you cannot be sure that the window will be kept open. When I went back to my mother, the window was barred, and there was another little boy sleeping in my cradle." At that thought, Wendy started up with a look of horror in her face: "Perhaps by this time, Mother may be in half-mourning," she exclaimed, and John and Michael felt they dared not stay another moment in the Never-Never-Never Land.

What would they do if they were too late in coming back, and found other children in their beds, other children being bathed and dressed by Nana? They must go home at once.

The Boys crowded round Wendy, imploring her not to leave them, but she was firm. Not only would she return with John and Michael, but she would take all the Boys with her, for her mother to adopt. The Boys, as soon as they heard themselves invited to come too, were as happy as larks. For now each of them would have a true mother in Mrs. Darling, and would live in a house like other boys. In a moment they were packing their baby clothes, and were ready to start on their journey.

Peter alone refused. He was miserable at the thought of losing Wendy, but he couldn't consent to grow old and have a beard, as he knew he must do if he left the Never-Never-Never Land.   Never, never, could he do that! There was nothing for him, then, but to stay behind. Wendy was as careful as a little mother in pouring out Peter's medicine, and made him promise faithfully to take it every night.

But suddenly there was a stamping overhead, and banging and a clashing, and a shouting, and a sound of heavy people wrestling and struggling to and fro. The Pirates had taken the Red Indians by surprise. The children heard the fighting, and listened like mice to the squalling of cats, as frightened as could be, while Peter waited with his sword. The battle was very soon over. The Redskins were

beaten and ran like hares, or crawled
dangerously wounded into the thickets.
The triumphant Pirates were left victori-
ous, though a little out of breath, close
above the children's heads.

Hook, their captain,
more wicked-looking
than ever, listened
at the mushroom
chimney. "If the
Indians have won,"
Peter was saying,
"they'll beat the
tom-tom."

"Aha!" thought Hook, and he picked
up a tom-tom that one of the flying Indians
had left behind, and sounded it loudly;
"rub-a-dub, rub-a-dub, dub, dub, dub."

"Hurrah!" shouted the children down
below. "An Indian victory!"

"All will be safe," said Peter. "You
may go now! Tink will show you the
way," and bidding a hurried good-bye

SEIZED BY ONE OF THE SWARTHY RUFFIANS

to Peter, away they all went up the stairways in the tree-trunks, out into the forest.

The Pirates were ready for them. As each child came above the ground, he was seized by one of the swarthy ruffians who stood waiting. One by one, and silently, they were captured and flung into boats and transported to the pirate ship, which had anchored in the lake close by.

Everything had been done so quietly that Peter was quite unaware of his friends' sad fate. He only knew that he was all alone, that Wendy had left him, and that she, and Michael, and John, and all the Lost Boys who had been his companions were on their way from the Never-Never-Never Land to the country of the ordinary people who wear tall hats and tail-coats as soon as they are old enough, and grow up one after the other. Poor Peter threw himself on his bed and sobbed himself to sleep.

Hook was still lurking about, for the one thing that annoyed him most was that Peter had not left the cave with the rest, and was as yet safe.

But in his wicked heart a wicked scheme had already risen by which he hoped to kill his enemy. He had carefully listened to Wendy's last words : " Be sure and take your medicine, Peter." Here was the Captain's last chance. Creeping down to the door of the cave, he stretched his long arm round the ledge just inside, and poured a few drops of deadly poison into the glass, and, with a grin of triumph on his ugly face, he threw his cloak over his shoulder and stole away.

" Tap, tap, tap." Somebody was knocking at the door. " Who's there? " asked Peter sleepily.

" Tap, tap, tap."

He got up and opened the door. Tinker Bell, tinkling excitedly, flew into the room. " The Pirates have captured them ! " she

PART V

THE PIRATE SHIP

THE PIRATE SHIP

THE pirate ship was a terribly evil-looking craft with its painted sails, its heavy tarred cordage, and its flag with the skull and crossbones upon it, flapping grimly at the stern. The poor children were at once driven into the dark and dirty hold, while Hook walked the deck, rubbing his hands and chuckling to himself to think that at last he had them in his power.

"Are all the prisoners chained so that they can't fly away?" he asked Smee, who was very busy at his sewing-machine.

"Aye, aye, Captain," answered Smee.

"Then hoist them up," shouted the Captain.

He seated himself on a chair covered
with a white bearskin, waiting while the
Boys, whose wrists were chained together,
were dragged out of the hold and brought
before him.   Six of them, he said, were to
walk the plank at once, but he would save
any two who were willing to be cabin
boys.   The children were not at first sure
what walking the plank meant, but Hook
soon enlightened them by roaring out a
song in explanation.

THE PIRATE SHIP

he sang, waving his hook to show how, when the plank tipped, they would be shot into the water and drowned.

Turning towards John Napoleon Darling he shouted: " You look as if you had some pluck in you ! " John hesitated. In his schoolboy days he had always thought a pirate's life very attractive, so stepping forward, he said: " Will you call me Red-handed Jack? " The Captain laughed with delight, and promised to give him that name if he joined the crew. Then Michael went up to him and slapped him on the shoulder. " What will you call *me* if I join? " he asked. " Black-Bearded Joe," answered the Captain, and until another question arose Michael was much pleased. The cabin boys were told that they must of course swear " Down with King George ! " and to this neither boy would consent. John and Michael were then pushed on one side and told that their doom was sealed, while

Hook shouted, "Bring up their mother."

In a moment Wendy was dragged from the hold, and when the Boys rushed to  protect her they were pulled back, leaving her standing alone, looking very frightened but pretty in her brown dress, with a long brown cloak wrapped round her. Hook asked her if she had any last message for her sons who were about to die. Wendy spoke beautifully to the Boys, telling them she was sure their real mothers would wish them to die like English gentlemen. Her courage so inspired the children that they all cried they would do what their mothers wished. Upon this, Wendy was cruelly tied to the mast whilst Hook's orders were being carried out.

But, just as the Boys' fate seemed determined, something happened to change Hook's glee into terror. " Tick! tick! ter-ick, tick, tick! " he heard, and at the dreaded sound he yelled : " The crocodile! hide me, hide me! " In abject fear he rushed to a corner of the ship while his men crowded round him, intent only upon shielding their captain from the jaws of the monster. The Boys, too, waited breathless with horror, until with sudden relief and rapture they saw not the crocodile but their beloved captain Peter Pan appearing over the ship's side. In one hand, at arm's length, he held an alarum clock, the ticking of which had made Hook believe that the crocodile was upon him.

Making a sign to his friends, Peter dashed into the cabin, unseen by the Pirates, and shut the door. The ticking ceased directly, and Hook's terror vanished.

Returning to his dreadful purpose he

cried: " Now here's to Johnny Plank! "
Again he began to sing, " Yo ho, yo ho,
the frisky plank," but the Boys, filled with
hope and excitement, drowned his voice
by singing " Rule, Britannia," and just
as the Pirate was about to vent his rage
upon them he was silenced by a shrill and
piercing cock's-crow from the cabin.

Struck motionless with terror, the crew
looked to their Captain for some explanation, who ordered Gecco, one of his men,
to enter the cabin and see what was the
matter. Hook waited, but Gecco did not
return, and once again was heard the awful
mysterious crowing. " Someone must
bring me out that doodledoo," roared the
Captain, and, as no one volunteered, "I
thought I heard Starkey volunteer," he
said, pointing his hook at Starkey. Mad
with terror of the hook as well as of the
uncanny creature in the cabin, Starkey
rushed wildly round the deck, and finally,
to escape both, flung himself overboard.

Furious at this mutinous behaviour, Hook shouted, " I'll bring that doodledoo out myself," but he had no better success, and came rushing back in a cowardly fashion, saying: " Something blew out the light."

A happy idea now struck him. " Drive the Boys in—let them fight the doodledoo —if they kill him so much the better, if he kills them we're none the worse."

This, of course, was just what the children wanted, but, concealing their delight, they allowed themselves to be driven into the cabin. In the meantime, all the Pirates huddled together, hiding their faces. Sailors, you know, are very superstitious, and they all thought the ship was bewitched. So terrified were they that no one saw Peter steal out, followed by the Boys, who crept silently up the ladder to the higher deck. No one saw Peter cut the ropes which bound Wendy, and take her place at the mast, and cover his face

F

with the brown cloak she had left, while Wendy joined the Boys.

"It's the girl!" cried Hook, "there's never luck on a pirate ship with a woman aboard; let's throw her over." All the men knew that their Captain was right, and one of the Pirates started up and shook his fist at the brown-robed figure at the mast. "There's nothing can save you now, Missy," he cried. "There is one," came a ringing voice, and the brown cloak was flung aside and there stood Peter Pan. "Down, Boys, and at them," he shouted, and with a rush the Boys, armed with weapons which Peter had found and given them in the cabin, swarmed down upon the lower deck. The Pirates believed that all the Boys had been slain by the mysterious doodledoo, and were panic-stricken as they saw them with swords and daggers. Some of the crew rushed to the bulwarks and leapt overboard; others with their knives fell upon the Boys, while

" That man is mine ! "

Hook backed into the cabin fighting for his life. " Put up your knives, Boys, that man is mine ! " cried Peter, pointing to Hook. The Boys turned their attention to the remaining members of the pirate crew, who were one by one forced into the sea, while the two mortal enemies appeared at the cabin door closed in deadly combat. Each was determined to kill the other. Step by step Hook was driven back to the side of the ship.   He felt himself weakening.   In despair he cried out : " 'Tis some fiend fighting me ǀ Who are you, Pan ? "

"I'm youth !" cried Peter, "I'm a little bird that has broken out of the egg.   I'm youth !   I'm joy !"
With that he wrenched Hook's sword from him

and pushed him into the sea, right into the jaws of the waiting crocodile, who caught him at last.

The Boys burst into ringing cheers as they and Wendy crowded round their hero, who stood like a conquering Napoleon while the pirate flag was lowered.

THE FATE OF THE PIRATES

All the pirates save two, Smee and Starkey, jumped into the sea and were drowned.

Smee, the Irish Pirate, who was not so wicked as the rest of the crew, managed to swim ashore, and subsequently became a reformed character and a brave sailor in His Majesty's Fleet.

Starkey, who had never shed blood, but had been guilty of many cruel deeds, was captured by the Redskins and led a miser-

RIGHT INTO THE JAWS OF THE CROCODILE

able life, for Great Big Little White
Panther, the Indian chief, compelled him
to act as nurse to the papooses of the
tribe—a sad come-down for a pirate!

HOME, SWEET HOME

BUT at home in the Darling household all this time there was deep sorrow. Mr. Darling, as a punishment to himself for taking their guardian Nana away, had vowed that he would live in the kennel till his children's return. For months now he had lived in it, and had been carried to business in it every morning, much to the disgust of the prim little housemaid Liza. Mr. Darling had become quite a celebrity, and great ladies, leaders of society, found him so interesting and touching, that they all cried out as he passed by, " Oh, do come to dinner at our house, do come in the kennel!" All the newspapers had asked him to write the cricket and football news for them, and his picture postcards were to be seen in every shop window.

But it happened one evening, when he returned from business, carried as usual in the kennel, he was taken up to the now desolate nursery, where Mrs. Darling spent most of her time mourning for her lost children, while the faithful Nana tried in vain to cheer her up. " George, George, I believe you are beginning to *like* that kennel," she said reproachfully, as he crawled out. He denied the charge, however, and tried to comfort Mrs. Darling, who never for one moment forgot the little empty beds and the silence and cheerlessness of the nursery. Then he left her, and sitting down by the fire, Mrs. Darling was alone with her sad thoughts.

tiny mauve, and white, and blue lights.
The mauve ones are boy fairies, the white,
girl fairies, and the blue lights are darling
little sillies who are not quite sure what
they are.

And the still air is filled with the singing
of birds and the ringing of hundreds of
little fairy bells. But the sweetest sound
of all is the fluting of Peter Pan's pipe as
he sits outside the little house and calls to
the spring to make haste, because with the
spring comes Wendy.